Whispers of the

Dream Granter

WHISPERS

OF THE

DREAM GRANTER

APRIL BIJOU

Copyright © 2025 April Bijou

All illustrations by April Bijou & Inhouse Productions

All rights reserved. No part of this publication may be reproduced, stored in a retrieval system, or transmitted in any form or by any means (including electronic, mechanical, photocopying, recording, or otherwise) without prior written permission from the publisher.

ISBN 9798218687021

Manufactured in the USA

APRILBIJOU.COM

BONBONAVENUE.COM

For Lewis Carol,

who opened the door to Wonderland.

At his grave, a dove startled the silence

and in its gaze, I felt his blessing.

A Note from the Author

This book is more than a story, it is a piece of my soul, lovingly stitched together in quiet moments between sunrises, stars, and the soft whispers of my heart. I wrote *Whispers of the Dream Granter* as a sanctuary, a place where wonder lives, where wishes bloom, and where every creature, no matter how small, is seen and cherished.

As April Bijou, I carry within me a deep love for animals, wildflowers, forgotten dreams, and the secret language of nature. The world of Bonbon Avenue Village came to life during my travels, in quiet hotel rooms, and high above the clouds, always pulling me back to a place of innocence, kindness, and believing in something beautiful.

This book is for the dreamers. For the soft hearts. For those who listen to the wind and find magic in the quiet.

May you always believe in wishes, and may this story be a gentle reminder that the greatest magic lives within you.

Not long ago, I carried Bunny with me to the grave of Lewis Carroll, the dreamer who opened the door to Wonderland. There, beneath the hush of centuries, I asked for his blessing for Bunny, for this story, for the dream about to take flight.

As I turned to leave, a sudden sound shattered the silence: the loud, unearthly flutter of wings. A dove burst from the tree beside his grave, alighting upon a nearby stone, and fixed me with its gaze. In that moment, I felt his presence unmistakable, gentle yet commanding. It was as though Carroll himself had spoken, not in words but in spirit, offering a wordless benediction.

And so, *Whispers of the Dream Granter* carries not only my heart, but the echo of his. A lantern lit one hundred and sixty years ago, now passed into new hands yours.

With all my heart,
April Bijou

Chapter I.
The Peculiar Breeze

Lily had always been an ordinary girl in an ordinary town, until the day a peculiar breeze swept through her bedroom window, carrying the scent of freshly baked cookies and blooming flowers. The wind tickled her nose and whispered in her ear, "Come, Lily. Bonbon Avenue Village awaits."

Startled, Lily turned to see her ornate bedroom mirror glowing faintly, as if moonlight had spilled across its surface. And then *clink!* a golden key tumbled from its center, landing softly at her feet. It shimmered like a forgotten star, delicate and old, yet strangely warm to the touch.

The moment her fingers closed around it, the mirror rippled like water. Without time to think, Lily was pulled forward, falling, tumbling through a swirl of pastel colors and twinkling lights. When she finally landed with a soft thud, she was no longer in her familiar bedroom but in the heart of a whimsical village unlike anything she had ever seen.

Whispers of the Dream Granter

Cobblestone paths meandered between charming cottages, each more colorful and curious than the last. The stones beneath her feet seemed to hum with a gentle warmth, as if greeting her arrival. The air was sweet with the mingling scents of perfume and pastries, and a symphony of cheerful chatter and tinkling laughter filled her ears. In the center of it all stood a majestic tree with shimmering leaves that seemed to dance in a non existent breeze, its branches swaying gently as if waving hello.

As Lily stood there, wide-eyed and heart racing, a white rabbit in a simple white dress with a cream colored cardigan and a yellow bow around her neck hopped up to her. The rabbit's nose twitched excitedly, and she balanced a tray of colorful perfume bottles on one paw with surprising grace.

"Oh my, oh my! You must be new here," the rabbit exclaimed, her voice as warm and comforting as a cup of hot cocoa. "Welcome to Bonbon Avenue Village! I'm Bunny, and I run the perfumery just down the lane. Would you like a whiff of 'Daydream Delight' or perhaps 'Whispered Wishes'?"

Lily blinked in surprise, her mind struggling to process the talking rabbit before her. "A talking rabbit? I must be

Whispers of the Dream Granter

dreaming!" she gasped, pinching herself to make sure she was awake.

Bunny giggled, her ears bobbing with amusement. "Dreaming? Perhaps. But in Bonbon Avenue Village, dreams have a funny way of coming true. Come along now, we mustn't dawdle. The Wish Granter is waiting!"

"The Wish Granter?" Lily asked, following Bunny down the winding path, marveling at how the flowers seemed to lean towards them as they passed.

"Why, the Dream Tree, of course!" Bunny exclaimed, pointing toward the shimmering tree in the village center. Its leaves rustled with anticipation, creating a melodious tinkling sound. "It's been whispering about your arrival for days. Something about a great adventure and a wish that needs granting."

As they approached the Dream Tree, Lily noticed other peculiar villagers gathering around. There was a badger in a blue apron dusted with flour Mr. Crumbles, the baker, who was absentmindedly kneading dough in mid-air. A graceful duck with impossibly long eyelashes was sipping tea

Whispers of the Dream Granter

Penelope from the tea house, her feathers shimmering like silk in the soft light. And then there was a clumsy frog wearing a green bow, Mr. Wobbles, who seemed to be tripping over his own feet every few steps, yet always managing to land with a cheerful "Oopsie-daisy!"

The leaves of the Dream Tree stirred, their shimmering rustle growing into a soft symphony. A voice drifted through the air, gentle yet full of warmth, as if carried by the wind itself. "Ah, Lily, welcome. It seems your heart has led you here, though you may not recall wishing for it. To find your way home, you must first lend your hand to our villagers in need. Only then, dear one, will the true nature of your wish unfold."

Lily's head spun with questions, her heart pounding with a mixture of excitement and trepidation. But before she could ask any, a blur of orange fur darted up to her. It was a mischievous fox with a green bow, his eyes twinkling with barely contained glee.

"First stop, my hidden den!" he declared with a wink, his tail swishing playfully. "I'm Felix Trotterfoot, and I've lost my favorite paintbrush. Without it, I can't finish my masterpiece!

Whispers of the Dream Granter

And let me tell you, it's going to be the talk of the village. Even more than Mr. Crumbles' floating cupcakes!"

With a deep breath and a heart full of wonder, Lily took her first step into this mysterious, enchanting world. The cobblestones beneath her seemed to hum with quiet encouragement, while the very air shimmered with unseen magic. Though unaware of the adventures and mysteries that awaited her, or the true wish hidden within, her spirit soared with the promise of extraordinary things just beyond the horizon.

Chapter II.
The Fox's Magical Map

Whispers of the Dream Granter

Lily followed Felix through the winding forest path, leaving the heart of Bonbon Avenue Village behind. The playful fox led her deeper into the woods, his green bow bobbing with each sprightly step.

As they walked, Lily noticed the trees whispering to one another, gossiping about her arrival. "Oh, look at her! She's new here, isn't she?" one tree murmured. "Yes, yes," another replied, "do you think she knows where she's going?"

"My den is just ahead," Felix announced, his bushy tail swishing excitedly. "It's a bit off the beaten path, but that's how I like it!"

As they approached a large, gnarled oak tree, Lily gasped. Nestled among the roots and lower branches was a whimsical door, painted in vibrant colors that almost camouflaged it against the forest backdrop. As Felix reached to unlock it, the door suddenly shrank to the size of a mouse hole, then expanded back to normal size, as if testing whether Lily was truly meant to enter.

"Welcome to my humble abode!" he exclaimed as they stepped inside.

Whispers of the Dream Granter

Lily's eyes widened in wonder. The den was a riot of color and creativity, but it seemed to play tricks on her perception. Canvases floated in mid-air, with paint blobs rearranging themselves into new images before her eyes. The colors from the paintings dripped off the canvases, forming small puddles on the floor that then reassembled into fantastic new landscapes.

Jars of paint in every hue imaginable cluttered shelves and tables. In one corner, a pile of seemingly random objects sparkled and gleamed Felix's treasure trove. Lily examined the curious items: a teacup that giggled when she picked it up, a spoon that muttered "Oh, do be careful!" when she touched it, and a mirror that showed not her reflection, but a window into what seemed to be another world entirely.

"Now, about that paintbrush," Felix mused, scratching his chin with a paw. Suddenly, a paintbrush appeared in his paw, only to dart away with a puff of glittery smoke. "Ah, there it is!" Felix exclaimed, reaching for it, but it vanished again with a mischievous twinkle. "Oh, never mind. Let me show you my special map!"

Whispers of the Dream Granter

He led Lily to a large canvas hanging on the far wall. It depicted an intricate, beautifully painted map of Bonbon Avenue Village. The details were exquisite: every cottage, shop, and landmark rendered in vivid color.

"Watch this," Felix said with a wink, picking up an ornate paintbrush. As he pointed it at different locations on the map, something magical happened.

When he touched the brush to the Whispering Woods, the trees in the painting began to argue, their branches flailing as they debated where they should be rooted. Next, Felix moved the brush to Bunny's Perfumery. Instantly, a cloud of animated perfume bottles erupted from the canvas, spritzing scents that temporarily turned the room purple and caused Felix to sneeze out a shower of rainbow sparkles.

"And look here," Felix said, touching the brush to Mr. Crumbles' Bakery. The painted bakery bustled with activity, but then something extraordinary happened. Cakes and pies floated off the canvas, tempting Felix, who tried to snatch them out of the air. "Come back here, you tasty morsels!" he cried, leaping after a particularly enticing éclair that darted just out of reach before diving back into the painting.

Whispers of the Dream Granter

As Felix's eyes lingered on the bakery, they suddenly gleamed with a mischievous light. He began rubbing his paws together eagerly, his tail swishing with barely contained excitement.

"Oh, I simply can't wait to show you the way to Mr. Crumbles' bakery!" Felix exclaimed, his voice drifting into a dreamy tone. "All those delicious cakes... the pies... the pastries!" He closed his eyes, almost salivating at the thought.

Lily noticed a subtle change in Felix's demeanor. There was something in the way his eyes darted about and his paws twitched that suggested he was hiding a delightful secret that he couldn't quite keep to himself.

"That sounds wonderful, Felix," Lily said, a hint of suspicion creeping into her voice. "But I thought we were looking for your paintbrush?"

Felix's ears twitched, and he quickly composed himself. "Oh, yes, yes, the paintbrush. Of course. But surely we can make a quick stop at the bakery first? For... inspiration! Yes, artistic inspiration!"

As they made their way back to the village and towards the bakery, Lily noticed strange occurrences around them. A few villagers were whispering and pointing at Felix, quickly looking away when he glanced in their direction. She could have sworn she saw Mr. Wobbles the Frog shaking his head disapprovingly... only to trip over his own feet when Felix waved at him.

The closer they got to Mr. Crumbles' bakery, the more agitated Felix seemed to become. His tail flicked nervously, and he kept glancing over his shoulder as if expecting someone to be following them.

"Are you okay, Felix?" Lily asked.

Just as they were about to round the corner to the bakery, a stern voice called out, "Felix Trotterfoot! Don't you dare take another step towards those cakes!"

Felix froze, his ears flattening against his head. Lily turned to see Bunny hopping towards them, her usually cheerful face set in a disapproving frown.

"Oh, hello Bunny!" Felix said with forced cheerfulness. "Lovely day for a walk, isn't it?"

Bunny crossed her arms. "Felix, you know very well that you're not allowed near Mr. Crumbles' bakery after what

Whispers of the Dream Granter

happened last time. Those cakes were for the Dream Tree ceremony!"

Lily's head was spinning with confusion. "What's going on?" she asked, looking between Bunny and Felix.

Felix's shoulders slumped, and he turned to Lily with a sheepish grin. "Well, you see, I may have a teensy habit of... borrowing... Mr. Crumbles' cakes," he shied. "For artistic purposes, of course! The way the frosting glistens is simply inspiring!"

Bunny snorted. "Borrowing? Is that what you call sneaking in through the chimney and making off with an entire three-tiered cake?"

As Felix scrambled to explain himself, Lily's thoughts wandered deeper into the strange mysteries of Bonbon Avenue. Why was Felix so fixated on the cakes? What exactly was this Dream Tree ceremony? And most puzzling of all, how did it all tie into her being here?

The Dream Tree's leaves whispered once more, and the gentle voice spoke with quiet wisdom: "Curiosity leads to knowledge, but be cautious, for not all is as it appears here in the village. To discover your true wish, Lily, you must first unravel the sweetest of mysteries..."

As the voice faded, a shiver of excitement ran through Lily. It felt as if she was stepping into an unusual adventure. Were cakes really more than they seemed? Did every villager have a secret? Smiling to herself, she wondered what topsy-turvy challenge would come next.

Whispers of the Dream Granter

Chapter III.
The Perfumed Path

Whispers of the Dream Granter

As Bunny lectured Felix about his cake-stealing habits, Lily's attention was drawn to a sweet, floral scent wafting through the air. It seemed to be calling to her, pulling her away from the commotion.

"I... I think I need to follow that scent," Lily said, her voice dreamy and distant.

Bunny's nose twitched. "Ah, you've caught a whiff of my latest creation! Come along then, let's leave this troublemaker to think about what he's done."

As they walked away, Felix called out, "I'll behave! Painter's honor!" But Lily noticed him crossing his fingers behind his back, a sly glint in his eyes.

The cobblestone path seemed to shift and change as they walked, colorful flowers sprouting between the stones with each step. Lily felt as if she were floating rather than walking, carried along by the intoxicating aroma.

"Here we are," Bunny announced, gesturing to a pastel cottage that was growing right out of a giant flower. "Welcome to my perfumery!"

Whispers of the Dream Granter

Inside, the air was thick with a rainbow of scents. Bottles of every shape and size lined the walls, each containing a differently colored liquid. In the center of the room stood a curious contraption of glass tubes and brass gears, bubbling and steaming.

"This is my Scent Synthesizer," Bunny explained proudly. "It can capture any smell and turn it into a perfume. But lately, it's been acting rather... peculiar."

As if on cue, the machine gave a great shudder and began to whistle. Colorful smoke poured from its spouts, filling the room with a dizzying array of scents. Lily caught whiffs of freshly baked bread, then spring flowers, then something that reminded her of old books and tea.

"Oh dear," Bunny fretted, hopping from lever to lever. "It's never done this before!"

Suddenly, the smoke began to take shape, forming into the silhouette of a squirrel. As the figure became clearer, Lily could make out a pair of bright, mischievous eyes.

"Willow Quicktail!" Bunny exclaimed. "What in the world are you doing in my Scent Synthesizer?"

The smoke-squirrel giggled, a sound like tinkling bells. "Just having a bit of fun, Bunny! Your machine caught me as I was leaping by. Did you know it can capture more than just smells?"

Before Bunny could respond, the smoke shifted again, this time forming the shape of a hedgehog.

"Oliver?" Lily asked, remembering the description from Felix's magical map.

The smoke-hedgehog nodded, his spines bobbing. "Hello there! Lovely day for a swim in scents, isn't it?"

Bunny looked as if she might faint. "But... but how did you both get in there?"

"Oh, that's simple," came a new voice, and the smoke swirled once more to reveal a pig with a large purple bow. "We followed the glittering trail!"

"Twiggy Winkle," Bunny sighed, shaking her head. "I might have known you'd be involved in this mischief."

As Lily watched in amazement, the smoke continued to shift and change, revealing more and more of Bonbon Avenue's residents. There was Eva the Lamb, her woolly coat sparkling with what looked like stardust. Winston Toadley appeared, reciting a poem about the scent of inspiration. Even Professor Whittleton made an appearance, adjusting his spectacles as he examined the inner workings of the Scent Synthesizer from the inside.

"This is extraordinary," Lily breathed, her head spinning with the impossible sight before her.

Bunny wrung her paws. "But how do we get them out? The Dream Tree ceremony is tonight, and everyone needs to be there in person, not as... scent spirits!"

The word 'ceremony' tickled something in Lily's memory. Hadn't Felix mentioned something about cakes for a ceremony? And the Dream Tree had spoken of tasks she needed to complete. Could this be one of them?

As if in response to her thoughts, the gentle voice of the Dream Tree whispered through the perfume-laden air: "To release your friends from their fragrant forms, you must uncover the scent that binds them. Only through this will the path to your deepest wish unfold before you."

Whispers of the Dream Granter

Lily glanced at the hundreds of bottles lining the walls, each filled with a different scent. Somewhere among them was the key to solving this puzzle. She took a deep breath, the mix of perfumes filling her lungs, and stepped forward, ready to face whatever challenge this strange little village had in store for her next.

Lily scanned the bottles, their vibrant colors twinkling like jewels on the shelves. Each one seemed to hum with energy, almost as if the scents within were alive. Her fingers hovered over them, her instincts guiding her to the right combination. "If it's the scent that binds them... maybe it's not just one," she murmured.

Bunny watched anxiously, her nose twitching as Lily began to pull bottles from the shelves. "Are you sure about this, Lily? Mixing scents is... delicate work."

Lily gave a small, determined smile. "I think this is why I'm here."

With steady hands, she selected a bottle that smelled faintly of roses, another of fresh rain, and a third of something warm and sweet, like cinnamon. She carefully poured them into the glass beaker at the heart of the Scent Synthesizer, watching as the liquids swirled together, changing colors in the process.

The machine sputtered for a moment, then let out a soft hum. Lily held her breath, her heart pounding. Slowly, the smoke that had formed the shapes of her new friends began to dissolve. One by one, the figures of Willow, Oliver, Twiggy, Eva, Winston, and Professor Whittleton shimmered back into their full, solid selves.

"Well done!" Winston croaked, his eyes twinkling with admiration. "A perfect blend of inspiration!"

Bunny clapped her paws, relieved. "You did it, Lily!"

Lily exhaled, a wide smile spreading across her face. "I guess I did."

Chapter IV.
The Midnight Masquerade

Whispers of the Dream Granter

As the excitement in Bunny's perfumery settled, Lily noticed the sky outside had turned a deep, velvety purple. Stars twinkled into existence, but they seemed to shine with an unusual, almost musical quality.

"Oh my!" Penelope the Duck exclaimed, her long eyelashes fluttering. "It's nearly time for the Midnight Masquerade!"

"The what?" Lily asked, her curiosity piqued.

Mr. Crumbles, who had just waddled in with a tray of colorful cupcakes, chuckled. "The Midnight Masquerade, my dear, is the prelude to the Dream Tree ceremony. It's when all of Bonbon Avenue comes alive with music, dance, and a touch of mystery!"

As if on cue, the cobblestone streets outside began to glow with soft, multicolored lights. Lily could hear the faint strains of an enchanting melody drifting through the air.

"But I don't have a mask," Lily said, suddenly feeling out of place.

Eva the Lamb stepped forward, her pink bow bobbing. "Not to worry, darling. I've been preparing for this moment!" With a flourish, she produced a shimmering mask that seemed to be woven from moonbeams and stardust.

As Lily put on the mask, she felt a tingle of magic wash over her. Her simple dress transformed into a gown that rippled with colors like the northern lights. Suddenly, a voice whispered in her ear, "Ah, finally! I've been waiting for a good face to wear!"

Lily jumped, startled. "Did... did you just speak?" she asked the mask.

"Of course I did, dear," the mask replied. "And may I say, you wear me quite well. Now, shall we dance?"

"Now you're ready for the ball!" Twiggy Winkle squealed, his large purple bow somehow even more vibrant in the magical atmosphere.

The villagers poured out onto the streets, each wearing a unique mask that reflected their personality. Wobbles the Frog hopped along in a mask made of water lilies, while Oliver the Hedgehog sported one that looked like a cluster of autumn leaves.

Whispers of the Dream Granter

As they approached the village square, Lily gasped in wonder. The Dream Tree stood at the center, its leaves shimmering with an inner light that pulsed in time with the music. Around it, fantastical creatures danced, some Lily recognized as villagers in elaborate costumes, others seemed to be living embodiments of dreams and wishes.

"May I have this dance?" asked a voice beside her. Lily turned to see Felix, wearing a mask that changed colors with every movement.

As Lily took his paw, she found herself swept into a dance that defied gravity. They twirled and spun, sometimes touching the ground, sometimes floating among the stars that had descended to join the festivities.

"Careful, don't step on that shadow. It's borrowed!" Lily's mask quipped as they narrowly avoided a patch of darkness.

"Felix," Lily said as they danced, "what is this ceremony everyone keeps talking about?"

Felix's eyes sparkled mischievously behind his mask. "Ah, nosy, are we? The ceremony's when the Dream Tree grants a

Whispers of the Dream Granter

wish. But here's the kicker: it's got to be one that's good for everyone. No asking for a lifetime supply of cakes, sadly."

As they continued to dance, Lily noticed something strange. With each turn, the dancers seemed to leave trails of glowing threads behind them. These threads began to weave together, forming a tapestry in the air.

"Look!" cried Winston Toadley, pausing in his poetic recitation. "The Tapestry of Wishes is forming!"

But this was no ordinary tapestry. It seemed alive, jumping and wriggling like a snake, singing softly in strange, whimsical harmonies as it formed. The threads argued amongst themselves as they wove together.

"No, no, Penny needs a new bookstore, not a bigger one!" one thread insisted.

"But what about my flying machine?" another chimed in before darting off in a random direction.

Lily watched in awe as images appeared in the glowing threads: a new wing for Penny's bookstore, a magical oven for Mr. Crumbles' bakery, a flying machine for Willow Quicktail's adventures. But the images kept morphing into strange and unpredictable forms: a smiling moon, a talking teapot, a pair of dancing shoes before settling into the real wishes.

Suddenly, a pie floated out of the tapestry and started dancing with the crowd. "That's my wish!" Felix exclaimed, trying to catch it, but it disappeared back into the fabric before he could grab it.

But there was a blank spot in the center of the tapestry, shimmering with potential.

"That, Lily, is where your wish will rest," came the soft, wise voice of the Dream Tree. "But before it can take flight, you must first uncover what it truly is."

Suddenly, the music changed. It became faster, more urgent. The dancers began to spin more quickly, their forms blurring together.

"The Whirlwind Waltz!" Benji Thistledown shouted over the music. "Hold on tight, everyone!"

Lily felt herself being pulled into the center of the dance. Colors swirled around her, faces flashed by in a dizzying array. She caught glimpses of all the villagers she had met, each one smiling encouragingly at her.

As the dance reached its crescendo, Lily found herself at the foot of the Dream Tree. Its branches seemed to reach down towards her, leaves brushing against her mask.

"The time has come, Lily," the Tree whispered. "What is your heart's true wish?"

Lily's mind raced. What did she want? What did Bonbon Avenue need? As she opened her mouth to speak, a sudden gust of wind swept through the square, extinguishing all the lights and plunging everything into darkness.

A collective gasp rose from the villagers. When the lights slowly faded back in, Lily saw that the Tapestry of Wishes had vanished. In its place floated a single, dark feather.

"Oh no," Bunny whispered, her ears drooping. "It can't be..."

"What?" Lily asked, a shiver running down her spine. "What's happening?"

Penny the Owl stepped forward, her wise eyes grave behind her star-shaped spectacles. But instead of speaking, she opened a book from her collection. To Lily's surprise, the pages spoke:

"Oh, dear. Shadows aren't supposed to come alive during the Masquerade," the book said in a worried tone. It continued, "An old shadow has returned. But is it really a shadow, or just a wish that's lost its way?"

As the villagers huddled together, whispering fearfully, Lily felt the weight of their hopes settle on her shoulders. Whatever this shadow was, she knew her adventure in Bonbon Avenue was far from over. In fact, it seemed the real challenge was only just beginning...

"Curiouser and curiouser," Lily's mask whispered, echoing her own thoughts as she faced the unknown that lay ahead.

Chapter V.
The Shadow's Whisper

Whispers of the Dream Granter

As dawn broke over Bonbon Avenue, the village was uncharacteristically quiet. The usual cheerful chatter and tinkling laughter were replaced by hushed whispers and worried glances. Lily, still wearing her shimmering gown from the Masquerade, found herself in the center of a gathering at The Wise Owl's Nook.

As they entered the bookstore, Lily gasped in wonder. Books were hopping off the shelves, dancing in circles around them. Some opened and closed like mouths, speaking in rhymes:

"The Shadow comes, the lights grow dim, but fear not, for I know you'll win."

Penny the Owl perched atop a stack of ancient tomes, her feathers ruffled with concern. "It's been many moons since we've seen a sign of the Shadow," she hooted softly.

Professor Whittleton adjusted his spectacles, flipping through a dusty volume. "Indeed, my dear. Not since the Great Dimming of years past."

"The Great Dimming?" Lily asked, her curiosity piqued despite the tense atmosphere.

Whispers of the Dream Granter

Willow Quicktail, her tail twitching nervously, piped up. "It was a time when all the colors in Bonbon Avenue began to fade. The Dream Tree's leaves turned gray, and wishes stopped coming true!"

Mr. Crumbles added, kneading dough in his paws, "Yes, and the Dream Tree had a dreadful time convincing the stars to come back. They were having a picnic on the moon!"

"But how did it end?" Lily pressed, looking around at the worried faces of her new friends.

A hush fell over the gathered villagers. Finally, Professor Whittleton stepped forward, his eyes twinkling with a mix of wisdom and absurdity. "The Wishkeeper? Ah yes, they traded their wish for a bucket of stardust and a teaspoon of dreams! Remarkably effective, if you ask me."

Before Lily could ask about the Wishkeeper, a cold wind swept through the bookstore, causing the pages of open books to flutter wildly. The wind rearranged books on the shelves, forming them into cryptic shapes like question marks and shadows of animals. In the swirling papers, Lily caught glimpses of strange symbols and ominous shadows.

Whispers of the Dream Granter

Suddenly, a voice that sounded like dry leaves scraping against stone whispered through the air: "A wish unspoken, a heart uncertain... such delicious doubt to feast upon!"

Wobbles the Frog, startled by the voice, tumbled off his chair, sending a cascade of books tumbling to the floor. But instead of falling, the books bounced around the room, popping like balloons. One book even scolded Wobbles: "Honestly, keep your feet in one place, dear!"

As the books fell, one landed open at Lily's feet. On its pages was an illustration of a creature made entirely of swirling darkness, with eyes that glowed like dying embers.

"The Shadowmancer," Penny gasped, her wings fluttering in agitation. "It feeds on doubt and unfulfilled wishes. If it's returned, all of Bonbon Avenue could fall into endless twilight!"

Lily felt a chill run down her spine. "But why now? Why is it back?"

Tilly Turtledove, who had been unusually quiet, suddenly hiccuped, and a small golden coin clinked to the floor. As everyone turned to look, the coin began to spin of its own accord.

"The balance has been disturbed," whispered the Dream Tree, its voice seeming to flow from the spinning coin itself. "A new Wishkeeper has come, yet her wish remains undefined. This uncertainty has opened a rift, through which the Shadowmancer begins to creep."

All eyes turned to Lily, and she felt the weight of their gazes. "Me?" she squeaked. "I'm the new Wishkeeper?"

Eva the Lamb placed a gentle hoof on Lily's shoulder. "It seems so, darling. Your arrival was no accident. The Dream Tree called you here for a reason."

Felix Trotterfoot, his usual cheeky grin replaced by a spark of determination, stepped forward. "Well then, looks like it's on us to help Lily figure out her wish! Can't have the Shadowmancer getting the upper hand, now, can we?"

A murmur of agreement rippled through the gathered villagers. Bunny's nose twitched with excitement. "We'll need to embark on a quest! To the farthest corners of Bonbon Avenue and beyond!"

Whispers of the Dream Granter

As the villagers began to chatter excitedly about preparations for the journey, Lily felt a mix of fear and exhilaration. She was still unsure about this whole Wishkeeper business, but looking around at the kind faces of her new friends, she knew she couldn't let them down.

Just then, Oliver the Hedgehog came bursting through the door, his spines quivering with excitement. "Everyone! Come quick! Something's happening at the Dream Tree!"

The villagers rushed out of the bookstore, Lily carried along with the tide of furry and feathered bodies. As they reached the village square, a collective gasp rose from the crowd.

The Dream Tree's leaves were slowly turning silver, and from its branches hung shimmering keys of various shapes and sizes. At the base of the tree, a door had appeared, a door that certainly hadn't been there before.

"The Doors of Destiny," Professor Whittleton breathed in awe. "I thought they were just a legend!"

Lily stepped forward, drawn by an invisible force. As she approached, one of the keys floated down from the tree and hovered before her. As it descended, it transformed, shifting from a feather to a spoon to a tiny cloud before finally settling into the shape of a key.

The Dream Tree's voice stirred softly among the leaves: "Behind each door lies a fragment of your true wish, Lily. But be on your guard, for the Shadowmancer will seek to lead you astray. Trust in your heart, and in the friends who walk this path with you."

As Lily reached for the key, she felt the eyes of all of Bonbon Avenue upon her. This was the beginning of her real adventure. With a deep breath, she grasped the key, its warmth spreading through her hand.

"Well," she said, turning to her friends with a mix of determination and nervous excitement, "I guess it's time to start unlocking some doors!"

And with that, Lily took her first step towards uncovering the mystery of her wish, and saving Bonbon Avenue Village from the encroaching shadows.

Chapter VI.
The Labyrinth of Lost Dreams

Whispers of the Dream Granter

As Lily grasped the shimmering key, the door at the base of the Dream Tree creaked open, revealing a swirling vortex of mist and starlight. She turned to her friends, a mixture of excitement and apprehension on her face.

"I... I think I need to go through alone," she said, somehow knowing it to be true.

Bunny hopped forward, her nose twitching anxiously. "But Lily, we can't just let you face the unknown by yourself!"

Felix Trotterfoot clapped a paw on Bunny's shoulder. "You know, sometimes the wildest adventures are the ones you've got to tackle solo," he said, his usual grin replaced by a rare flicker of wisdom.

With a deep breath, Lily stepped through the doorway. As soon as she crossed the threshold, the door vanished behind her with a puff of confetti. A sign appeared out of nowhere, reading: "Welcome! No refunds, no shortcuts!"

Lily found herself standing at the entrance of an enormous labyrinth, its walls shimmering with an opalescent light.

"Welcome, Wishkeeper, to the Labyrinth of Lost Dreams," came a voice that seemed to change with every word. Lily turned to see a talking mirror floating before her, its reflection constantly shifting. One moment it showed Lily's face, the next she was wearing a giant hat, then a rabbit mask.

"Oh, I'm not really here, but neither are you! Welcome, or was it goodbye?" the mirror Guardian chuckled.

"Who are you?" Lily asked, awestruck.

"Guardian of this realm, that's me," the mirror purred, its surface rippling. "You'll face trials here, uncovering pieces of your true wish. But watch the shadows... the Shadowmancer lurks in the dark."

As the Guardian faded away, Lily noticed that the labyrinth walls were not solid, but rather composed of swirling images and half-formed thoughts. She recognized snippets of her friends' wishes from the Tapestry Mr. Crumbles' magical oven, Penny's expanded library.

Taking a deep breath, Lily began to navigate the twisting paths. As she walked, she heard whispers and glimpsed shadowy figures just at the edge of her vision. The air grew

Whispers of the Dream Granter

thick with the scent of Bunny's perfumes, then shifted to the aroma of Mr. Crumbles' baked goods.

Suddenly, she came upon a clearing where three paths diverged. At the entrance to each path stood a shimmering apparition:

To the left was a version of herself, dressed in the finest clothes, surrounded by adoring fans. "Choose me," it said, "and you'll have fame and admiration beyond your wildest dreams."

The path in the center showed Lily surrounded by piles of gold and jewels. This version spoke in rhyme:

"Choose me, and you'll never grow old,

For life is made easy when bathed in gold!"

But as Lily watched, the gold began to melt and reform into strange shapes, like castles made of marshmallows.

But it was the right path that gave Lily pause. There she saw herself, older and somehow wiser, surrounded by the smiling faces of her Bonbon Avenue friends. This Lily held a glowing orb in her hands, which seemed to pulse with the hopes and dreams of the entire village.

Whispers of the Dream Granter

As Lily pondered her choice, a shadow fell across the clearing. The silky voice of the Shadowmancer whispered in her ear, "Why choose just one? Take them all! Think of the power you could wield..."

For a moment, Lily felt tempted. But then she remembered the warmth of her friends, the magic of Bonbon Avenue, and the trust they had placed in her.

With renewed determination, she stepped onto the right-hand path. As soon as she did, the other apparitions vanished, and the path before her lit up with a warm, golden glow.

She continued on, facing more challenges, riddles posed by spectral versions of Professor Whittleton, agility tests that would have made Willow Quicktail proud, even a baking challenge judged by an illusory Mr. Crumbles. As she progressed, the Labyrinth itself seemed to help her, with paths magically widening or flowers pointing her in the right direction while humming a cheerful tune.

With each trial overcome, Lily felt a piece of understanding click into place within her heart. Her true wish was taking shape, though it remained just out of reach.

Whispers of the Dream Granter

Finally, she arrived at the labyrinth's center. There, floating in a pool of liquid starlight, was a single jigsaw puzzle piece made of pure light.

As Lily reached for it, the Shadowmancer's voice hissed once more, "Turn back, Wishkeeper. Some truths are too painful to face."

But Lily stood firm. "I'm not afraid," she declared. But as she reached for the puzzle piece, it darted away playfully.

A voice like tinkling bells asked, "What's small, round, and always glowing, even when it's not?"

Lily thought for a moment, then smiled. "A wish!" she exclaimed.

The puzzle piece spun in the air, then zoomed towards her hand. As her fingers closed around it, she felt a surge of warmth and understanding.

In a flash of blinding light, Lily found herself back in Bonbon Avenue, standing before the Dream Tree. Her friends gathered around her, eyes wide with wonder.

"You did it!" Bunny exclaimed, hopping with joy.

Lily opened her hand, revealing the glowing puzzle piece. As the villagers gazed upon it, their eyes filled with hope.

"It's beautiful," breathed Penelope the Duck, "but what does it mean?"

Lily's eyes lit up with a bright spark. "So it means we're getting closer to beating the Shadowmancer and saving Bonbon Avenue! But... we still have a lot to do, don't we?"

As if in response, another key materialized from the Dream Tree's branches, hovering before Lily.

"The next door stands before you, dear Wishkeeper," the Tree murmured gently. "The time has come to unveil yet more secrets... are you prepared?"

Lily looked around at her friends, drawing strength from their supportive smiles. "I am," she said firmly, grasping the new key. "Whatever challenges lie ahead, we'll face them together."

And with that, the magical denizens of Bonbon Avenue prepared for the next phase of their grand adventure, the fate of their whimsical world hanging in the balance.

Chapter VII.
The Clockwork Carnival

Whispers of the Dream Granter

As Lily grasped the new key, the air shimmered and twisted. In the blink of an eye, she and her closest companions - Bunny, Felix, and Wobbles - found themselves standing at the entrance of a fantastical carnival. Towering clockwork contraptions whirred and spun, their gears gleaming in the ethereal light.

"The Clockwork Carnival!" Bunny gasped, her nose twitching. "I thought it was just a legend!"

Felix chuckled, his tail swishing. "Oh, it's real, alright. And if the stories are true, it's where time itself gets a little… playful."

As they spoke, the clockwork contraptions burst into song, their gears and cogs forming melodies that rhymed and intertwined. A nearby Ferris wheel groaned, "I've been turning backward for centuries! Can't someone just let me go forward for once?"

Wobbles, trying to steady himself on the shifting ground, gulped nervously. "P-play? That doesn't sound ominous at all…"

Whispers of the Dream Granter

As they ventured into the carnival, Lily marveled at the sights around her. Carousel horses galloped through the air, their manes made of flowing ribbons of light. Ferris wheels turned backwards, their passengers aging in reverse. Candy floss stands spun treats that tasted like memories, and ring toss games used halos of time instead of rings.

"Step right up! Step right up!" called a voice that sounded like the ticking of a thousand clocks. They turned to see Tilly Turtledove, dressed in a ringmaster's outfit, standing atop a podium. "Welcome to the Clockwork Carnival, where past, present, and future collide! Are YOU brave enough to face the Timekeeper's Challenge?"

Lily stepped forward, feeling the puzzle piece from the labyrinth grow warm in her pocket. "What's the challenge?" she asked.

Tilly's eyes sparkled with a strange light. "It's simple, really. You just need to find your true wish in the Hall of Mirrors. But be careful time doesn't play fair there, and the Shadowmancer's whispers only get louder the longer you stay."

Whispers of the Dream Granter

With a hiccup, Tilly produced a golden pocketwatch. Inside, the grains of sand were tiny dancing figures, making a show of falling slowly or speeding up. "You have until the last grain of sand falls through this hourglass. Fail, and you'll be trapped in a moment for all eternity."

Bunny gasped. "That's too dangerous! There must be another way!"

But Lily felt a surge of determination. "No, I have to do this. For Bonbon Avenue, for all of you."

As Lily neared the Hall of Mirrors, Felix called out, "Lily! Just remember, things aren't always what they seem in there. Trust your heart!"

The moment Lily stepped into the Hall of Mirrors, the world around her fractured into a thousand reflections. Each mirror showed a different version of herself - past, present, and possible futures. The mirrors shifted sizes and wobbled like jelly, with some versions of Lily stepping out of their frames before darting back in.

She saw herself as a child, playing in Bunny's perfume garden. In another, she was helping Sophie design magnificent dresses for a grand Bonbon Avenue ball. Some reflections showed her in fantastic scenarios exploring uncharted lands with Willow Quicktail, or solving ancient puzzles with Professor Whittleton.

But as she delved deeper into the hall, darker reflections began to appear. She saw versions of herself consumed by greed, by fear, by loneliness. The Shadowmancer's whispers grew louder, trying to lure her towards these darker paths.

One mirror showed Lily surrounded by gold and jewels, laughing in an exaggerated, echoing voice. As she watched, the treasures melted into puddles, reforming into strange shapes like dancing teacups.

"Why fight it?" the shadow hissed. "Embrace the darkness, and all these futures could be yours."

Lily felt herself being pulled in all directions, lost in the maze of possibilities. Time seemed to stretch and contract around her. Was she moving forward or backward? Had she been here for minutes or years?

Just as despair began to creep in, she caught a glimpse of something in a distant mirror. It was herself, but not alone.

Whispers of the Dream Granter

She was surrounded by her Bonbon Avenue friends, all working together to create something beautiful. Tiny floating orbs containing the laughing faces of her companions surrounded this version of Lily, as if they were already cheering her on. In her hands, she held a glowing orb that seemed to contain the essence of the Dream Tree itself.

"That's it!" Lily gasped. "My true wish... it's not just about me. It's about all of us, about keeping the magic of Bonbon Avenue alive!"

The moment she spoke these words, the mirrors around her shattered, exploding into confetti which turned into tiny gears and clocks that giggled and bounced around. As the shards fell, they reformed into another puzzle piece, fitting perfectly with the one she already had.

Suddenly, Lily found herself back at the carnival entrance, her friends rushing to embrace her.

"Oh, thank goodness!" Bunny exclaimed, hopping up to Lily. "I thought you were going to stay in the carnival forever! The mirrors might have made you a ringmaster!"

Whispers of the Dream Granter

"You did it!" Wobbles cheered, promptly tripping over his own feet. But before he could fall, shards of broken mirrors from the Hall of Mirrors formed a helpful cushion, bouncing him back up.

Tilly Turtledove appeared, a proud smile on his face. "Well done, Wishkeeper. You've passed the Timekeeper's Challenge and taken another step towards uncovering your true wish." He hiccupped, sending out golden coins that floated around Lily, forming a shimmering halo.

As the carnival began to fade around them, returning them to Bonbon Avenue, Lily felt a new sense of purpose. She may not have fully formed her wish yet, but she now understood its essence - it was about connection, about preserving the wonder and magic of this extraordinary place.

Back in the village square, the Dream Tree's leaves rustled with approval. Another key materialized, hovering before Lily.

"The final challenge lies ahead," the tree murmured softly. "Are you prepared to confront the Shadowmancer and claim your true wish?"

Whispers of the Dream Granter

Lily looked at her friends, then at the two puzzle pieces she had earned. The pieces glowed and twirled around each other, offering encouragement in playful tones: "Don't worry, Wishkeeper. We've got this!"

With a determined nod, she grasped the key. "I'm ready," she said. "Let's save Bonbon Avenue, together."

As the key turned in an invisible lock, the air around them began to darken. The final confrontation was about to begin, and the fate of Bonbon Avenue hung in the balance.

Chapter VIII.
The Shadow's Embrace

Whispers of the Dream Granter

As the darkness swirled around them, Lily and her friends found themselves transported to a realm unlike anything they had seen before. The once vibrant colors of Bonbon Avenue were muted, as if viewed through a veil of gray mist. The air was thick with whispers that formed actual words, floating past Lily's head and muttering things like "Watch your step!" and "Careful with those wishes!"

"Welcome, little Wishkeeper," came a voice that seemed to echo from everywhere and nowhere at once, sometimes laughing maniacally, then whispering riddles. "Welcome to my domain."

Before them materialized a figure that seemed to be made of living darkness. Its eyes glowed like dying embers, and its form shifted constantly, never quite settling on a single shape. One moment it was a giant cat with glowing eyes, the next it melted into a puddle only to reform as a tower of shadowy teacups.

"The Shadowmancer," Bunny whispered, her ears drooping in fear.

Benji's ears, usually so expressive, lay flat against his head. "It's even scarier than I imagined," he murmured.

Whispers of the Dream Granter

The Shadowmancer's laugh was like the rustling of dead leaves. "Oh, I'm so much more than your fears, little ones. I am doubt, I am despair, I am every unfulfilled wish and broken dream. And oh, the fun we could have together!"

Lily stepped forward, the puzzle pieces glowing warmly in her pocket. "We're not afraid of you," she declared, though her voice trembled slightly. "We've come to save Bonbon Avenue."

"Save it?" the Shadowmancer mocked, morphing into a giant shadowy cake. "Why save something so small, so insignificant? I can offer you worlds, little Wishkeeper. Entire realms of shadow where you could reign supreme. You could have the power to bend time! Imagine... endless tea parties! Or days where you only have dessert for breakfast!"

As it spoke, the air around them shimmered, showing visions of vast, dark kingdoms. Lily saw herself seated on a throne of shadows, powerful and feared. But the visions were bizarrely whimsical - Bunny trapped in a giant hatbox, Benji endlessly chasing his own ears, and Mr. Crumbles attempting to bake but with all his ingredients floating away.

Whispers of the Dream Granter

Sophie Willowtail gasped. "Lily, don't listen! Remember who you are, remember Bonbon Avenue!"

The Shadowmancer hissed, and the visions changed. Now Lily saw her friends trapped in cages of darkness, their joy and color slowly draining away. "This is the fate that awaits them if you refuse me," it threatened, its voice suddenly serious before breaking into a giggle.

Lily felt fear grip her heart, but then she remembered the warmth of the Dream Tree, the laughter in Mr. Crumbles' bakery, the wonder of Felix's magical paintings. She thought of Wobbles' endearing clumsiness, Benji's excitable ears, and Sophie's kind smile.

"No," Lily said, her voice growing stronger. "Bonbon Avenue isn't insignificant. It's a place of wonder and magic, of friendship and dreams. And I won't let you destroy it!"

As she spoke, the puzzle pieces in her pocket began to glow brighter. Lily pulled them out, and to her amazement, they floated in front of her, spinning around each other like dancing fireflies. They giggled and hummed a tune as they fused into a glowing sphere of light.

Whispers of the Dream Granter

The Shadowmancer recoiled. "What is this? What are you doing?"

Lily reached out and grasped the orb, which bounced playfully in her hand. "Oh, don't mind me, I've been waiting to light up your world!" it said cheerfully.

As she held the orb, Lily felt the hopes and dreams of all of Bonbon Avenue flowing through her. She saw Penelope hosting her elegant tea parties, Willow Quicktail embarking on daring adventures, and Eva the Lamb designing beautiful dresses. She felt the wisdom of Penny and Professor Whittleton, the creativity of Winston Toadley, and the nurturing spirit of Lila Belle.

"My wish," Lily said, her voice ringing with certainty, "is for Bonbon Avenue to always be a place of magic and wonder, where dreams can come true and friendship conquers all shadows!"

The orb in her hands exploded with light, driving back the darkness. The Shadowmancer howled, its form dissipating like mist in the morning sun.

Whispers of the Dream Granter

As the light faded, Lily and her friends found themselves back in the heart of Bonbon Avenue. The colors were brighter than ever, the air filled with the scent of flowers and freshly baked treats. The Dream Tree stood tall and proud, its leaves shimmering with newfound vitality.

Bunny hopped over and twirled like a ballerina. "Oh, Lily, you've brought back all the fun! I was worried we'd be stuck with gray hats forever!"

"You did it, Lily!" Benji exclaimed, his ears shooting straight up in excitement. "You saved us all!"

Felix tapped his nose with a cheeky grin. "I knew you'd pull it off! But next time, let's aim for more cake and fewer shadows, alright?

As the villagers gathered around, cheering and celebrating, the gentle voice of the Dream Tree spoke once more, its leaves shimmering like sparkling confetti: "Well done, Lily. Your true wish has been revealed and granted. Bonbon Avenue will forever be protected by the power of your friendship and imagination. Oh, and perhaps next time, don't trust the shadows they've been known to cheat at hide-and-seek!"

Whispers of the Dream Granter

Lily looked around at her friends, old and new, and felt a warmth in her heart. She may have started this journey as an ordinary girl, but here, in this extraordinary village, she had found a place where she truly belonged.

"So," Felix said with a mischievous grin, "ready for your next adventure?"

Lily laughed, feeling lighter than air. "Always," she replied. "After all, in Bonbon Avenue, the adventure never really ends, does it?"

And as the sun set on another magical day in the village, Lily knew that while she had unlocked the mystery of her wish, there were still countless wonders waiting to be discovered in the enchanted world of Bonbon Avenue.

Chapter IX.
The Everglow Festival

Whispers of the Dream Granter

As the days passed in Bonbon Avenue, the village seemed to shimmer with a new, vibrant energy. The defeat of the Shadowmancer had ushered in an era of unprecedented creativity and joy. To celebrate their victory and honor Lily's wish, the villagers decided to host the grandest event in Bonbon Avenue history: The Everglow Festival.

On the morning of the festival, Lily awoke to find a beautifully crafted invitation slipped under her door. It was adorned with Eva the Lamb's elegant calligraphy and Sophie Willowtail's intricate embroidery.

As Lily stepped outside, she gasped in wonder. The entire village had been transformed. Strings of luminous flowers, crafted by Bunny's expert paws, draped between the cottages. These flowers sang in harmony as they swayed in the breeze, occasionally switching places with each other on a whim, and even whispering secrets to the villagers as they passed underneath.

Mr. Crumbles and Hazelnut had outdone themselves, creating a towering cake that not only changed flavors with each bite but also shape-shifted depending on who was looking at it. One moment it was a multi-layered tower, the next a floating cake shaped like a swan that sailed gently through the air.

Penelope's tea house had expanded into an open-air café, serving beverages that sparkled like liquid starlight. The teacups hopped to different tables, insisting they'd found "the perfect spot" before settling down with a satisfied hum.

"Lily! Lily!" Benji Thistledown came bounding up, his ears flopping excitedly. "You won't believe what Felix and I have prepared for the festival!"

Before Lily could ask, Benji grabbed her hand and led her to the village square. There, she saw an enormous canvas stretched between two trees. Felix, paintbrush in hand, was adding the finishing touches to a mural that seemed to move and change as she watched.

"It's a magical memory canvas," Felix explained, his tail swishing proudly. "Touch any part of it, and you'll relive a moment from our adventures!"

Lily reached out and brushed her fingers against a swirl of color. Instantly, she found herself momentarily transported back to the Clockwork Carnival, now complete with marching cupcakes. Another touch, and she was at the Midnight Masquerade, dancing with a smiling moon.

As she pulled away, the canvas itself chuckled. "Oh yes, that was a fabulous adventure! Do you remember the part with the flying teapot? Classic!"

As the day progressed, more wonders unfolded. Willow Quicktail had set up an obstacle course that defied gravity and logic. Visitors not only leaped and bounded through the air but also walked upside down, ran backward in time, and floated through hoops made of rainbows. "Oh, well done!" one obstacle cheered. "But watch out for the flying hats up ahead; they can be a bit cheeky!"

Tilly Turtledove hiccupped a shower of golden coins that transformed into butterflies, fluttering through the crowd and granting small wishes to whoever they landed on. The butterflies giggled and hummed little tunes, their wings changing colors depending on the wish they granted. One landed on Lily's shoulder and whispered, "How about a dance with the stars next?"

Even Wobbles the Frog had a special role. His clumsiness had been turned into an asset, as he led a group of giggling children in a "topsy-turvy dance" where the goal was to be as endearingly uncoordinated as possible. The more off-balance the dancers became, the more gravity itself began to warp causing dancers to spin into the air, float sideways, or even slide across invisible floors. Wobbles himself tripped over his feet and ended up gracefully floating upside down, much to everyone's delight.

As twilight approached, Professor Whittleton called everyone to gather around the Dream Tree. "My dear friends," he announced, adjusting his spectacles, "it's time for the grand finale of our Everglow Festival!"

Penny the Owl stepped forward, carrying a delicate lantern crafted from spun moonlight. "Lily," she said warmly, "would you do us the honor?"

With trembling hands, Lily took the lantern. As if guided by an unseen force, she knew exactly what to do. She closed her eyes, focused on her wish for Bonbon Avenue, and gently blew into the lantern.

A soft, warm light began to emanate from it, growing brighter and brighter. Suddenly, streams of luminescent color

Whispers of the Dream Granter

burst forth, swirling around the gathered villagers and up into the branches of the Dream Tree.

The Tree's leaves began to glow, each one a different hue, creating a dazzling display that lit up the night sky. The glowing leaves took on different shapes, some resembled floating stars, others looked like tiny creatures made of light. From these magical leaves, tiny sparks of light began to fall, each one carrying a small wish or dream.

"Oh my!" exclaimed Lila Belle, as a spark landed on her nose, granting her wish for a new herb garden. The herbs sprang to life in a whimsical way, singing lullabies and floating slightly above the ground.

"Woohoo!" cheered Twiggy Winkle, as another spark swirled around him, creating a flurry of bubbles that sang as they floated, each one popping with a tiny musical note.

All around, villagers laughed and cheered as their small wishes unfolded in surprising ways. The air buzzed with magic, music, and a sense of camaraderie.

Whispers of the Dream Granter

As Lily watched her friends celebrate, she felt a gentle tap on her shoulder. She turned to see Winston Toadley, a thoughtful smile on his face.

"You know, my dear," he said, his voice melodious, "I've been composing a poem about our adventures. Would you like to hear it?"

Lily nodded eagerly, and Winston cleared his throat. As he spoke, the words of his poem floated out of his mouth, turning into glowing butterflies and tiny musical notes that circled above the villagers' heads, creating a visual tapestry to accompany his poetry:

"In Bonbon Avenue, where dreams take flight,

A Wishkeeper came, banishing the night.

Through labyrinth and carnival, her spirit bright,

She taught us all the power of wish and sight.

Now colors dance and friendship reigns,

In this village where magic never wanes.

For in each heart, a dream remains,

Whispers of the Dream Granter

Nurtured by love, it grows and sustains.

And now, dear friends, a final note

Don't forget to thank your talking coat!"

As Winston's words faded, replaced by the cheerful bustle of the festival, Lily felt a sense of completion. She had not only found her place in this magical world but had also helped ensure that Bonbon Avenue would always be a haven of wonder and joy.

The Everglow Festival continued long into the night, a celebration of all that made Bonbon Avenue special. And as Lily danced with her friends under the glow of the Dream Tree, she knew that while this adventure might be ending, countless more were just waiting to begin in the enchanted world she now called home.

Chapter X.
Through the Perfume Glass

Whispers of the Dream Granter

As the Everglow Festival wound down, Lily found herself wandering back to Bunny's perfumery, drawn by a curious scent that seemed to dance just at the edge of her perception. The cottage, usually so quaint and orderly, now appeared to be swirling with mists of a thousand colors.

"Curiouser and curiouser," Lily muttered to herself.

She pushed open the door, which emitted musical notes that floated in the air like tiny birds, each singing a different tune before flying out the window. Inside, bottles and vials of every shape and size lined the walls, but they seemed to be shifting and rearranging themselves when Lily wasn't looking directly at them. The walls subtly shifted like puzzle pieces, with bottles hopping from one shelf to another, giggling softly. Lily even heard them whispering to one another, "I'm pure adventure! What about you?"

"Oh, Lily! You're just in time," came Bunny's voice, though the rabbit herself was nowhere to be seen. "We're about to begin the Olfactory Odyssey!"

"The what?" Lily asked, peering around a corner only to find it stretched impossibly long, like a tunnel made of fragrant mist.

Whispers of the Dream Granter

Suddenly, Benji Thistledown came hopping down this misty corridor, his ears twirling like propellers, causing him to hover above the ground. "It's a journey through scent and memory!" he exclaimed, his feet never quite touching the ground. "But mind the gaps, or you might fall into yesterday's perfume! Oh, and mind the ceiling, it likes to play tricks!" He added before doing a somersault midair.

Before Lily could ask what he meant, the floor beneath her feet began to change texture unexpectedly, transforming into a giant patchwork quilt made of smells. Each step released a different fragrance: laughter, vanilla dreams, rainbow clouds. Suddenly, the floor became transparent, revealing an ocean of swirling, fragrant liquid. She yelped in surprise, only to find herself gently floating downwards, as if gravity had decided to take a holiday.

As Lily floated down, the air filled with floating chairs and teacups that waved as they passed by, encouraging her to "Come join the dance!"

"Welcome to the Essence Emporium," came Mr. Crumbles' voice. The badger appeared, floating by on a giant macaron. "Care for a bite? It tastes like your fondest wish!"

Whispers of the Dream Granter

Lily took a nibble, and suddenly her mouth was filled with the flavor of starlight and dreams. She giggled, the sound turning into bubbles that floated upwards, each one containing a tiny scene from her adventures in Bonbon Avenue.

"Don't let them pop!" warned Sophie Willowtail, who was using her needle and thread to stitch the very air around them into fantastic shapes. As Sophie stitched, the shapes took on personalities of their own. A stitched cat spoke in rhymes, "Mind the thread, mind the loop, or you might end up in a soup!" The thread itself jumped from Sophie's needle and tried to tie itself around Lily playfully before being pulled back with a laugh.

As Lily swam through the perfumed sea, she encountered more of her friends, each engaged in impossible tasks that somehow made perfect sense in this topsy-turvy world. Felix was painting scents onto the air, creating invisible masterpieces that could only be experienced through smell. "You have to smell it to see it, darling!" he explained, waving a brush of perfume that filled the air with visual scents. "Ah, there's the perfect shade of 'Mischief in Spring!'"

Whispers of the Dream Granter

Penelope was hosting a tea party where the cups were made of solidified laughter, and the tea changed flavor with each sip. The cups giggled each time they were picked up, changing flavor based on what made the drinker happiest. "Oh, delightful! This one's 'sunshine with a dash of giggle,' and that's 'moonlight with a pinch of mystery,'" Penelope exclaimed. Each sip of tea caused tiny, glowing bubbles to rise from the drinker's nose, popping to reveal little puffs of music notes or miniature tea kettles that floated off into the distance.

"But where's Bunny?" Lily wondered aloud.

"To find the white rabbit, you must follow your nose," came the Dream Tree's voice, though it seemed to be coming from a tiny acorn floating past.

Lily closed her eyes and inhaled deeply. She caught a whiff of carrot cake, fresh flowers, and something indefinably magical. Following this scent, she swam deeper and deeper into the perfumed ocean.

Finally, she emerged in a bubble-like chamber where Bunny sat at an enormous distillery, her paws moving in a blur as she mixed and matched essences. Bunny's paws were mixing

Whispers of the Dream Granter

scents that changed into unexpected shapes, a daisy became a butterfly, a raindrop morphed into a tiny star, all while Bunny cheerfully hummed an off key tune.

"Ah, Lily! You've made it," Bunny said with a smile. "Tell me, what is the scent of a wish?"

Lily opened her mouth to say she didn't know, but instead found herself answering, "It smells like the laughter of friends, the pages of an unread book, and the first star of evening."

Bunny clapped her paws in delight. "Precisely! And that's the final ingredient we needed for the Everglow Elixir. With this, the magic of our festival will last all year round!"

As Bunny added a drop of Lily's words to her concoction, the entire perfume-glass world around them burst into a cacophony of colors, scents, and sound. Notes of music floated around like butterflies, bottles danced, and the walls rippled like water.

With a gentle pop, Lily found herself back in Bunny's cottage, everything seemingly back to normal. But there was a new bottle on the shelf, labeled "Everglow Essence", that sparkled with an inner light.

Bunny appeared beside her, looking as if she'd never left. "Quite a journey, wasn't it?" she said with a wink. "Now, shall we rejoin the others? I hear Wobbles is about to attempt a tightrope walk over a pool of Felix's color-changing paint. It promises to be quite the spectacle!"

As they stepped out into the perpetual twilight of the Everglow Festival, Lily couldn't help but wonder what other impossible adventures awaited her in this enchanted place she now called home. The world of Bonbon Avenue felt fluid and ever-shifting, with the boundaries between reality and dream always soft, as if any moment could turn into another adventure. In the distance, Lily spotted a floating doorway that seemed to wink at her, inviting her into the next fantastical journey. In Bonbon Avenue, it seemed, the line between reality and dreams was as thin as the gossamer wings of Tilly's golden butterflies, and just as magical.

Chapter XI.
The Seamstress's Spell

Whispers of the Dream Granter

As the Everglow Festival continued its enchanted revelry, Lily found herself drawn to a quaint cottage on the outskirts of Bonbon Avenue. The windows glowed with a soft, ever-changing light, and the scent of lavender and fresh linen wafted through the air.

"Sophie Willowtail's Atelier," Lily murmured, recognizing the intricate needlework on the sign above the door. The sign constantly changed fonts, at one point even shaping itself into a needle sewing into the wood.

As she reached for the doorknob, it suddenly turned towards her and spoke, "About time you arrived! Now, let's see what you can stitch together!" before opening with a dramatic bow.

Lily gasped at the sight before her. The walls of the atelier grew larger, warping into new shapes like giant buttons and safety pins. In the center of the room, suspended in mid-air, was the most beautiful dress Lily had ever seen. It shimmered with an otherworldly light, its colors shifting like the northern lights. As Lily approached, the dress hummed softly and glowed brighter, as if responding to her presence. The fabric shimmered, showing little scenes that changed depending on Lily's mood or touch.

Whispers of the Dream Granter

Scissors snipped at invisible threads, whispering, "Oh, I do love snipping away at mysteries!" Needles danced through the air, and spools of thread unwound themselves as if by magic, performing a quirky waltz.

"Oh, Lily! You're just in time," came Sophie's melodious voice, though the rabbit herself was nowhere to be seen. "The dress is almost ready. Why don't you step closer and take a look?"

Mesmerized, Lily approached the floating garment. As she did, she felt a strange tingling sensation. Suddenly, the room began to stretch around her, like an elastic space, with walls and floor bending as if made of soft fabric. Objects around her giggled and shifted sizes, mimicking her transformation as she shrank to the size of a thimble.

"Oh my!" Lily exclaimed, now standing on the hem of the dress itself. The fabric bounced under her feet like a trampoline, and she landed in a patch of stitching that acted like a soft, shimmering net.

"Welcome to the world within the seams," Sophie's voice echoed around her. "Every stitch is a story, every thread a path. Why don't you explore?"

Whispers of the Dream Granter

Lily set off across the fabric, marveling at how each section seemed to come alive as she touched it. The skirt was a vast meadow of silk flowers, each petal as big as Lily herself. She climbed a mountain of intricate lace, slid down rivers of satin ribbon, and swung from buttonhole to buttonhole like vines in a jungle.

As she journeyed, Lily encountered magical creatures born from loose threads and wayward sequins. A dragonfly with wings of gossamer lace gave her a ride over a sea of sequins, speaking in a butler's accent, "Please mind your step, madam, we've got a lot of stitching to do!" A family of mice made from softly glowing pearls showed her a shortcut through a forest of embroidered leaves.

At the bodice of the dress, Lily found herself in a grand ballroom made of mirrors and crystal beads. The mirrors shifted and rippled like pools of water, reflecting not just Lily, but strange, alternate versions of herself Lily as a ballerina, Lily as a queen of fabric and thread. Shadowy figures performed strange, gravity defying dances, spinning on the ceiling or waltzing through the air as they whispered fragmented memories of past wearers of the dress.

Whispers of the Dream Granter

As Lily twirled, the crystal beads above chimed like little bells, each one humming a different note, creating a dreamlike melody as the dance continued.

"You're doing wonderfully, Lily," Sophie's voice encouraged. "But remember, every dress has its secrets. Can you find this one's hidden treasure?"

Intrigued, Lily began to search more carefully. She peered under collars, investigated pockets, and examined every seam. In one pocket, she found a miniature umbrella that opened on its own. In another, a spool of thread tied itself into tiny animals. She even discovered a tiny tea set with cups that sloshed as if still full of invisible tea.

Finally, in the very heart of a beautifully embroidered rose, she found it - another piece of the puzzle she'd been collecting throughout her adventures. As she reached for it, the rose bloomed into a talking flower, offering cryptic advice: "Ah, you found me! But have you thought about the color of tomorrow's breeze?"

Just as her fingers closed around the puzzle piece, Lily felt herself growing once more. The world around her spun in reverse, with the creatures and objects waving as they shrank back to their original sizes. The dragonfly saluted, saying, "Until next time, brave adventurer of stitches and seams!"

In the blink of an eye, she was back to her normal size, standing in Sophie's Atelier with the completed dress before her.

Sophie appeared, riding on a floating pin cushion. "Bravo, dear!" she exclaimed, beaming with pride. "You've danced through the seams like a master! Care for a celebratory ribbon?"

The atelier itself seemed to respond, with threads dancing in the air, scissors snapping in applause, and buttons hopping on the shelves in celebration.

Lily looked down at the puzzle piece in her hand, then back at the dress. "It's beautiful, Sophie. Thank you for letting me be a part of its creation."

"The pleasure was all mine, dear," Sophie replied, her eyes twinkling. "Now, why don't you try it on? After all, a dress is meant to be worn, not just admired."

As Lily slipped the dress over her head, she felt the magic of her journey within its folds wrap around her. The dress adjusted itself with a mind of its own, the fabric rippling and shimmering, as if getting comfortable. It gave a soft sigh, saying, "Ah, perfect fit let's make magic together!"

It fit perfectly, as if it had been made for her all along - which, in a way, it had. The puzzle piece in her pocket hummed softly, as if excited to join the rest of the puzzle, offering encouragement like, "Onward to more threads of adventure!"

"Perfect," Sophie declared. "Now you're ready for whatever adventure comes next."

Lily twirled in her new dress, the puzzle piece safely tucked in its hidden pocket. As she thanked Sophie and prepared to rejoin the Everglow Festival, she couldn't help but wonder what other magical experiences awaited her in Bonbon Avenue, and how much closer she was to solving the mystery of the puzzle.

With excitement bubbling inside her and a dress full of magic, Lily stepped back into the whimsical world of Bonbon Avenue, eager for her next adventure.

Chapter XII.
The Clockmaker's Conundrum

Whispers of the Dream Granter

As Lily stepped out of Sophie's Atelier, her new dress shimmering with every movement, she noticed the air around her seemed to thicken. The sounds of the Everglow Festival became muffled, and a curious ticking noise filled her ears.

"Tick-tock, tick-tock," it went, growing louder with each passing second.

Suddenly, a pocket watch zipped past her nose, its chain trailing behind it like a metallic tail. It paused mid-air, its face turning to Lily as if studying her. "Keep up, keep up!" the watch chimed. "Time waits for no bunny!"

"Oh my, oh my! You're late, you're late!" came a familiar voice. Lily turned to see Benji Thistledown hopping towards her, his floppy ears now resembling the hands of a clock. The ears ticked and spun uncontrollably, making him hop in random directions. "Oh dear, my ears are running five minutes fast again!" he exclaimed, occasionally tripping over his own lagging shadow.

"Late for what?" Lily asked, bewildered.

Whispers of the Dream Granter

"For the Timeless Tea Party, of course!" Benji exclaimed, his ears spinning wildly. "Quick, follow that watch!"

Without warning, the pocket watch zoomed off, and Lily found herself chasing after it, her magical dress flowing behind her like a river of starlight. Benji bounded alongside, his clockwork ears tick-tocking with each hop.

As they raced through Bonbon Avenue, the world around them began to warp. The path beneath their feet rippled like waves, sometimes pulling Lily's feet forward or backward as if she were walking on time itself. They passed Mr. Crumbles' Bakery where cakes were un-baking themselves back into bowls, and through Penelope's Tea House where guests were drinking their tea upwards from their saucers into their cups.

Along the way, villagers started moving in reverse, speaking in backwards sentences. Lily found she could only understand them when she spun in place, "rewinding" their words.

Finally, they arrived at a towering grandfather clock in the middle of a clearing. Its face was a swirling vortex of numbers and symbols, and its pendulum swung in impossible directions, changing course every time someone blinked.

Whispers of the Dream Granter

"Welcome to the Chronomancer's Clocktower!" announced a voice from above. Lily looked up to see Tilly Turtledove perched atop the clock, wearing a waistcoat covered in tiny, ticking timepieces. Each clock chimed at different times, singing a different note or making a strange sound; one barked, another meowed, and one hiccupped every time Tilly spoke.

"I'm so glad you could make it," Tilly said, hiccupping a shower of golden gears that floated around, giggling like mischievous children and playing hide-and-seek with Lily. "We're in quite a pickle, you see. Time's gone all wonky, and we need your help to set it right!"

Lily stepped closer to the clock, her dress rippling with colors that seemed to match the swirling vortex on its face. "What do I need to do?" she asked.

Tilly gestured to the clock's face, where numbers were changing positions, forming little puzzles. "You must navigate the Maze of Minutes and find the Pendulum of Perpetuity. Only then can we restore the proper flow of time to Bonbon Avenue."

Whispers of the Dream Granter

With a gulp, Lily reached out and touched the clock's face. In an instant, she was pulled into the vortex, tumbling through a kaleidoscope of ticking clocks and whirling calendar pages.

She landed softly in a world where clock hands formed the ground, shifting beneath her feet and moving her forward and backward in time. Giant hourglasses created archways overhead, turning upside down and causing the world to flip with them. The sand falling inside whispered riddles that Lily had to solve before it ran out, or the hourglass would flip again.

As Lily navigated this clockwork landscape, she encountered various challenges. A puzzle master made of clock parts asked her a riddle: "What gets bigger the more you take away from it?" But when Lily tried to answer, the riddle changed depending on the time displayed on his watch.

Throughout her journey, Lily's magical dress proved invaluable. It flowed like liquid when she slipped through narrow gears, and at times it stopped entirely, freezing in place as if caught in a time loop. "Oh dear, looks like I'm stuck in yesterday!" the dress would say before starting to flow again. When Lily needed protection, the dress turned into

Whispers of the Dream Granter

whimsical armor made of spinning gears and ticking clock faces, each piece humming a different tune as it defended her from falling clock hands.

Finally, after what felt like hours (or was it merely seconds?), Lily reached the center of the maze. There, suspended in mid-air, was the Pendulum of Perpetuity, its gentle swing hypnotic and soothing. It vanished and reappeared at random points in time, forcing Lily to time her approach perfectly.

As she reached for it, the pendulum spoke, "Ah, a wishkeeper! What are you doing meddling with time? Naughty, naughty!" before allowing her to grasp it.

As Lily reached for it, she noticed something glinting at its base. It was another puzzle piece! The piece appeared and disappeared in random moments, and Lily had to catch it with a quick swipe.

The moment her fingers closed around them, the world around her began to spin. Clocks whirled, gears clicked, and hourglasses flipped. Lily saw multiple versions of herself at different moments in time before everything clicked back into place. With a great "BONG!" Lily found herself back outside the Clocktower, the pendulum in one hand and the puzzle piece in the other.

Tilly clapped his flippers in delight. "Splendid job, my dear! You've saved time itself!"

Benji hopped excitedly, his ears now back to their floppy selves. "Oh, it's good to have my old ears back, these clock ears were giving me a headache!" he exclaimed. "And just in time for tea!"

As Lily handed the pendulum to Tilly, she felt the puzzle piece warm in her hand. She carefully tucked it into the hidden pocket of her dress, alongside the others she had collected.

The air around them seemed to relax, and the sounds of the Everglow Festival returned to normal. Yet Lily couldn't shake the feeling that with each puzzle piece she found, she was getting closer to uncovering a greater mystery.

"Come along now," Tilly said, leading the way. "I believe Mr. Crumbles has prepared a special clock-shaped cake to celebrate!"

Whispers of the Dream Granter

When they arrived at the bakery, they found a marvelous clock-shaped cake that ticked like an actual clock, with hands made of chocolate moving in real-time. Every time someone took a bite, it ticked backward, causing everyone to briefly relive the moments just before their bite. As they ate, the cake announced the time, saying things like, "Oh, dear! It's tea time! No, wait, it's adventure time!"

As Lily followed her friends, her magical dress twinkling in the eternal twilight of Bonbon Avenue, she wondered what other time-bending, reality warping adventures awaited her in this enchanted village she now called home.

Chapter XIII.
The Whispering Woods

Whispers of the Dream Granter

As the celebration of restored time wound down, Lily found herself drawn to the outskirts of Bonbon Avenue. The twinkling lights of the Everglow Festival faded behind her, replaced by the soft, mysterious glow of bioluminescent mushrooms and fireflies.

"The Whispering Woods," Lily murmured, remembering Felix's magical map. She hadn't ventured this far before, but something about the forest called to her.

As she stepped between the first trees, her magical dress shimmered, adapting to the new environment. It took on the patterns of dappled sunlight through leaves, helping her blend seamlessly into the forest.

The trees greeted her in hushed, whispering voices: "Ah, the Wishkeeper arrives," said one. "Took her long enough," murmured another. A particularly tall tree leaned down and said, "Keep an eye on the mushrooms they like to gossip."

Bioluminescent mushrooms giggled softly and moved whenever Lily tried to look at them, giving her cryptic advice like, "Watch out for the tree that tells riddles it cheats!"

"Welcome, Wishkeeper," came a voice that seemed to emanate from the trees themselves. Lily turned to see Willow Quicktail, the clever squirrel, perched on a branch above her. "We've been expecting you."

"We?" Lily asked, looking around.

Willow giggled, her tail twitching mischievously. "The forest, of course! Every tree, every leaf, every root has a story to tell. And today, they want to share their secrets with you. The forest has been talking about you. It loves to chat, but don't take everything too seriously, especially the roots. They hold grudges."

The forest echoed Willow's giggles as if the entire place was alive, watching and interacting with Lily.

With a graceful leap, Willow led Lily deeper into the woods. As they traveled, Lily noticed the trees seemed to shift and move, creating paths where none existed before and closing off others. Some trees grew teacups as fruit, which occasionally tipped over and spilled their contents into the ground, creating small pools of tea.

Whispers of the Dream Granter

They soon arrived at a clearing where an enormous, ancient tree stood. Its trunk was gnarled and twisted, forming natural staircases and hideaways. Nestled in its branches were tiny treehouses, connected by rope bridges and vine swings.

"This is the Elder Oak," Willow explained. "It's the heart of the Whispering Woods and the keeper of all forest memories."

The Elder Oak seemed to be in the middle of a lively conversation with its own branches. "Hush, hush!" it said, "I'm about to make an important announcement," to which a branch replied, "We've heard this before!"

As Lily approached, the tree's leaves began to rustle, forming words: "Ah, the Wishkeeper. You're right on time... or perhaps you're late? Time doesn't work quite the same in here, you know." The leaves chimed in with comments like, "You missed tea, but you're early for dessert!"

"Greetings, young Wishkeeper. Are you ready to uncover the forest's deepest secret?" the Elder Oak asked.

Lily nodded, both nervous and excited.

Whispers of the Dream Granter

"Then listen closely," the tree whispered, its branches creaking as they bent down towards her. But just as Lily leaned in to hear its secrets, the tree suddenly straightened up, its leaves shaking with what sounded like laughter.

"Not so fast, young one!" The Elder Oak boomed. "Before I share my secrets, you must tell me a riddle. One that I haven't heard in at least a hundred years!"

As Lily pondered, other trees tried to help poorly. One tree shouted, "It's an umbrella!" while another insisted, "No, no, it's obviously a teapot." Meanwhile, a bush giggled and whispered, "They always get it wrong."

Finally, Lily stumped the Elder Oak with her riddle. The tree dramatically exclaimed, "Impossible! I haven't been stumped since the time a rabbit tricked me into thinking it was night during the day. Very clever of you. You've earned the right to hear my secrets."

The tree began to share its memories with Lily. As she climbed its branches, they rippled and became stairs made of stardust. Each memory played out like a living scene around her. Butterflies made of old memories fluttered past her, whispering fragments of forgotten dreams.

Whispers of the Dream Granter

Near the top of the tree, in a hollow bathed in soft, golden light, Lily found what she had been unconsciously seeking - another puzzle piece. As she reached for it, the piece glowed softly and hummed, almost like it was singing to itself. "Ah, I was wondering when you'd get here," it said as Lily touched it. "It's quite cozy being part of the big picture, you know."

"You've done well," the Elder Oak's voice rumbled. "You've shown yourself worthy of the forest's trust. Ah, another step closer! Soon, you'll know everything, but will you be ready for the answer?" it teased with a rustle of laughter.

Willow appeared beside her, eyes sparkling. "And you've uncovered another piece of your own puzzle! But be careful, Lily. The more pieces you gather, the closer you get to a choice that will change everything."

As they made their way back to the edge of the woods, Willow skipped alongside Lily, offering strange advice. "Oh, the forest told me a secret, don't trust the daisies. They're always up to something," she said with a wink. "Now that you've found another puzzle piece, things might get... twisty. Keep your eyes open and your feet on the ground, unless the ground decides to take a walk."

Whispers of the Dream Granter

Emerging from the Whispering Woods, Bonbon Avenue spread out before her, still aglow with the magic of the Everglow Festival. The trees rearranged one last time, forming the word "Goodbye!" before parting to reveal the path back. The mushrooms waved their caps, and the fireflies spelled out cryptic messages like, "See you next dream!" and "Don't forget the clocks!"

As Lily rejoined the festivities, she noticed the surroundings still carried hints of the Whispering Woods' playful magic. Lanterns in the village winked at her as if sharing a secret. Teacups on a nearby table started dancing for no reason, and flowers waved to her as she passed by.

One last whisper from the Whispering Woods echoed in her ear, saying, "Remember, the puzzle might not be what it seems... or maybe it is!"

Yet, as she rejoined the festivities, a small part of her couldn't help but wonder: when the puzzle was complete, would it lead her back to her old home? And if it did, would she want to go?

With these thoughts swirling in her mind, Lily stepped back into the twinkling lights of the festival, ready to embrace

Whispers of the Dream Granter

whatever magical adventure came next in her journey through Bonbon Avenue.

Whispers of the Dream Granter

Chapter XIV.
The Midnight Maze

Whispers of the Dream Granter

As Lily left the Whispering Woods, the puzzle piece from the Elder Oak warm in her pocket, she noticed the eternal twilight of Bonbon Avenue had deepened into an unusually dark night. The stars above twinkled with an intensity she had never seen before, forming constellations that seemed to move and dance.

"Curious," she murmured, her magical dress shimmering in response to the starlight.

Suddenly, a book appeared, its pages fluttering open as words wrote themselves in glowing ink. From these floating pages emerged Winston Toadley, the intellectual toad. His spectacles glinted in the starlight as he regarded Lily with a mix of excitement and concern. In his hand, a quill pen never stopped writing, leaving strange, nonsensical phrases in the air like, "Time flies, but where is it flying to?"

"Ah, Lily! Just the Wishkeeper we need," Winston said, his voice lyrical even in its urgency. "The Midnight Maze has appeared, and only you can navigate its ever-changing paths."

Before Lily could ask for clarification, the ground beneath her feet began to shift. Hedges sprouted from nowhere, growing at an impossible speed until they towered above her. The hedges hummed little tunes and swayed to the rhythm of the stars. Each one offered Lily advice that made no sense "Follow the starfish!" or "Look for the key in a lockless door!"

The stars overhead rearranged themselves into an arrow, pointing deeper into the newly formed labyrinth.

"Remember," Winston called as the hedges began to separate them, "in the Midnight Maze, logic is rarely logical, and the only constant is change!"

With those cryptic words, Lily found herself alone at the entrance of a vast maze. The hedges were not made of ordinary leaves and branches, but of shadows and starlight. They whispered secrets as she passed, some profound, others nonsensical.

As she ventured deeper, Lily encountered challenges that defied reason. One moment she was bouncing on a path that had become a trampoline, the next she was paddling through a river of stars with a giant spoon provided by a friendly bird with a pocket watch.

Whispers of the Dream Granter

She came upon a garden where flowers debated whether cake was a soup or salad. A particularly stubborn tulip insisted it was "neither," but rather "an idea," leaving Lily to ponder what that could possibly mean.

Another path turned her upside down, forcing her to walk on the star-studded sky while the ground loomed menacingly above. The starry sky started talking to her in riddles, each star twinkling out a word, while the upside-down ground mocked her attempts to solve it.

Her magical dress proved invaluable, adapting to each bizarre situation. When it transformed into wings to help her cross a chasm, it complained, "I'm not a fan of heights!" making Lily laugh as it fluttered its fabric in protest. When faced with a riddle telling sphinx made of mist, the dress whispered answers in rhyme, its starry patterns rearranging into helpful clues.

At the heart of the maze, Lily found a clearing where the laws of physics seemed to have taken a holiday. Objects floated freely, changing size and shape at random. A teapot scolded a clock, saying, "You're five minutes late for tea!"

Whispers of the Dream Granter

while a balloon floated past, offering cryptic advice like, "To catch the sun, you must first find its reflection."

In the center stood a sundial, despite the lack of sun, its shadow spinning wildly and zig-zagging unpredictably. The sundial laughed softly, saying, "Chase me if you can, but I always slip away!"

As Lily approached the sundial, she noticed something lodged in its center - another puzzle piece! But every time she reached for it, the sundial's shadow would whisk it away to another part of the clearing.

"Time is an illusion, and so is space," came the voice of the Midnight Maze itself, sounding like a thousand whispers speaking at once. "To claim your prize, you must be everywhere and nowhere, all at once. You must think like a cloud or be as slippery as jelly on a hot day."

Lily pondered this impossible task, watching as the puzzle piece danced just out of reach. Then, an idea struck her. She closed her eyes, took a deep breath, and focused on the magic of her dress. She imagined herself shrinking down into a single star, then expanding into a constellation, dancing through the sky. With each blink, she slipped between

Whispers of the Dream Granter

moments, stretching time like taffy until it no longer held her back.

To her amazement, she felt herself stretching, not painfully, but as if she were a thought expanding to fill the entire maze. For a brief, wondrous moment, Lily was aware of every path, every challenge, every star that made up the Midnight Maze.

When she opened her eyes, the puzzle piece was in her hand, and the maze around her was fading like mist in the morning sun.

She found herself back at the entrance, Winston Toadley beaming proudly at her. He snapped his fingers, causing tiny fireworks shaped like question marks to burst in the air, each one asking an impossible question, "What's the sound of a color?" or "How long is a piece of time?"

"Splendid job, my dear!" Winston exclaimed, presenting her with a clock-shaped cupcake. "You've saved us ten minutes and gained a puzzle piece, what a profitable endeavor!"

As Lily added the new puzzle piece to her collection, she felt a surge of excitement and apprehension. The puzzle piece hummed a little tune as it nestled into her pocket, whispering, "I've been waiting for this journey; it's much more fun than being lost in a maze!"

The night sky above began to lighten, returning to the familiar twilight of Bonbon Avenue. Yet Lily sensed that with each piece of the puzzle she collected, with each impossible challenge she overcame, she was moving closer to a moment of truth, a decision that would shape not just her fate, but perhaps the fate of this entire magical realm.

As the stars rearranged themselves into playful shapes like teapots and rabbits, giving Lily a final wink before fading, Winston, with a twinkle in his eye, said, "Ah, dear Lily, I do wonder what peculiar adventure awaits you next. Just remember, sometimes it's the questions with no answers that are the most important."

With a mixture of anticipation and nervousness fluttering in her heart, Lily set off back towards the village center, ready for whatever whimsical adventure awaited her next in the ever-surprising world of Bonbon Avenue.

Chapter XV.
The Carousel of Memories

Whispers of the Dream Granter

As Lily made her way back to the heart of Bonbon Avenue, the familiar sounds of the Everglow Festival reached her ears. However, there was something different in the air - a haunting melody that seemed to weave between the usual cheerful tunes.

Following the mysterious music, Lily found herself in a clearing she hadn't noticed before. There, bathed in an ethereal glow, stood a magnificent carousel. But this was no ordinary merry-go-round; instead of horses, it boasted fantastical creatures from the depths of imagination. Each one seemed to shift and change as she looked at them, never settling on a single form.

As Lily approached, the creatures whispered to her, each trying to convince her to choose them. "Pick me!" said a creature that was part cloud, part cat, and part teapot. "I'm practically perfect!" Another declared, "I'll take you on a journey made entirely of jelly!"

The creatures morphed into absurd combinations - a rabbit with fish scales, a dragonfly with a hat and monocle, and a bear made of cake. They bickered amongst themselves, arguing about whose journey was more exciting.

Whispers of the Dream Granter

"Ah, you've found it," came the gentle voice of Penny the Owl, who glided down to perch on a nearby branch. "The Carousel of Memories. It only appears when a Wishkeeper is close to completing their journey."

Lily's hand instinctively went to her pocket, feeling the weight of the puzzle pieces she'd collected. "What does it do?" she asked, her voice barely above a whisper.

Penny's eyes twinkled with wisdom. "It shows you what was, what could be, and what never was at all. But don't take anything too seriously, except when you should!" She paused, then added, "Choose wisely, but remember, the wisest choice isn't always the one that makes the most sense. In fact, it's usually the opposite."

As if responding to Penny's words, the Carousel began to spin slowly, its melody growing louder. Lily felt drawn to it, her feet moving of their own accord.

"Choose wisely," Penny called as Lily approached the Carousel. "Each creature offers a different journey through memory."

Whispers of the Dream Granter

Lily's eyes were drawn to a shimmering creature that seemed to be part unicorn, part butterfly, and part starlight. As she climbed onto its back, the world around her dissolved into a swirl of colors and sounds.

The world blurred into a kaleidoscope of colors, where time bent and stretched. Trees grew backwards, and stars swung like chandeliers, casting light that changed shape. Lily found herself not just observing memories, but interacting with them.

She stepped into Mr. Crumbles' kitchen to help bake a cake, only to find the ingredients singing opera and the dough tap-dancing across the counter. In Felix's studio, she tried to paint alongside him, but the paintbrushes had minds of their own, painting impossible things like "the sound of a whisper" and "the taste of purple."

As she experienced Willow Quicktail's first adventure, the trees cheered as if they were spectators at a sports game, holding up signs that said "Go Willow!" and "Climb faster!" Willow laughed and responded, "Oh, these trees, such drama queens."

Whispers of the Dream Granter

She watched the Dream Tree grow from a sapling, accompanied by a chorus of singing leaves, each one harmonizing about the wonders of Bonbon Avenue. One particularly out-of-tune leaf interrupted: "I prefer jazz, actually."

With each memory, Lily understood more about the magical realm she had come to love. She saw how each resident, each magical occurrence, was intricately connected to the others, creating a tapestry of wonder and friendship.

As the carousel spun faster, Lily's own memories began to intermingle with those of Bonbon Avenue. She remembered her life before, the ordinary world she had left behind. But now, those memories seemed pale in comparison to the vibrant experiences she'd had in this enchanted village.

Just as the whirl of memories threatened to overwhelm her, Lily noticed something glinting at the center of the Carousel. There, spinning on its own axis, was the final puzzle piece. As she reached for it, it flitted away at the last second, laughing and saying, "Catch me if you can!"

The sundial joined in the game, spinning faster as it said, "Time waits for no one! Except on Tuesdays."

Whispers of the Dream Granter

Lily realized she had to convince the puzzle piece to come to her. With a smile, she recited, "I'll never forget to thank my teacups before drinking!"

With a surge of determination, Lily reached out. The moment her fingers touched the piece, the Carousel came to a gentle stop, and she found herself back in the clearing.

As she climbed down, still dizzy from the rush of memories, Lily realized something had changed. Her magical dress, which had adapted to every adventure, now shimmered with scenes from all the memories she had experienced. A cake frosted itself on her skirt, while Felix's paintings leapt off her dress for a moment, hanging in midair before returning.

"Well, that was fun!" the dress commented. "I wonder if we'll get wings again soon?"

Penny flew down to her side. "You've done it, Lily. You've collected all the pieces of the puzzle. Now comes the moment of truth."

With trembling hands, Lily took out all the puzzle pieces. They seemed to vibrate with energy, eager to be united. As

Whispers of the Dream Granter

she began to fit them together, each connection sent a spark of magic into the air.

When the final piece slid into place, there was a flash of blinding light. When Lily could see again, she gasped. Floating before her was a key, unlike any she had ever seen. It sparkled with all the colors of Bonbon Avenue, and seemed to hum with pure magic.

"The Key of Wishes," Penny said solemnly. "With it, you can unlock the door back to your old world. But be warned, using the key is a choice that cannot be undone. You must decide where your heart truly belongs."

The key spoke in rhyme, "I unlock doors to worlds unknown, where dreams and secrets have been grown. But choose with care, dear Wishkeeper bold, for once unlocked, the tale is told!" It hummed a little tune as it floated in the air, winking at Lily as if sharing a private joke.

Lily stared at the key, her mind whirling with possibilities. The air around her rippled, showing quick flashes of what might await her in both worlds, glimpses of her life before Bonbon Avenue mixed with playful visions of what staying might hold, like dancing teapots, talking animals, and stars that tell stories.

The Dream Tree chimed in, whispering, "Wherever you go, there's always more to know."

As the weight of the decision settled upon her, Lily realized that her greatest adventure and her most difficult choice still lay ahead.

Chapter XVI.
The Crossroads of Lost Destiny

Whispers of the Dream Granter

As Lily stood there, the Key of Wishes hovering before her, the entire world of Bonbon Avenue seemed to hold its breath. The eternal twilight deepened, casting long shadows that danced and swirled around her feet. In the distance, the Dream Tree's leaves rustled with anticipation.

"Lily," came a chorus of voices. She turned to see all her friends from Bonbon Avenue gathering around her. Bunny, Felix, Wobbles, Benji, Sophie, and all the others, each face filled with a mixture of love, hope, and sadness.

Mr. Crumbles stepped forward, a bittersweet smile on his face. "We've known this moment would come, dear Lily. The choice has always been yours to make."

As if summoned by his words, two doors materialized on either side of Lily. One was her bedroom door from her old world, familiar and ordinary. The other was a whimsical creation that seemed to embody the very essence of Bonbon Avenue, ever-changing, sparkling with magic and possibility.

The doors began to speak, each trying to persuade Lily. The ordinary door said in a proper, businesslike voice, "Come on, hurry up! Life awaits! No time for nonsense." The magical door whispered, "Ah, but nonsense is where the heart truly lives, isn't it?"

The doors began to bicker. "She's not staying here! She's far too ordinary!" the magical door huffed. "Ordinary? Why, she's the most extraordinary person I've ever met!" the ordinary door retorted.

Penny the Owl fluttered between them, saying, "Oh, hush, you two. Lily needs to think."

The Key of Wishes pulsed gently, waiting for Lily to make her decision. It floated around playfully, making Lily chase it as it said, "Catch me if you can! I'm the key to everything, but also nothing at all!" As Lily finally caught it, it murmured, "What unlocks doors but never turns? Isn't it funny how some keys open doors and others lock hearts?"

Penelope the Duck spoke up, her voice gentle but filled with whimsy. "Remember, Lily, there's no right or wrong choice. Only the path that feels true to your heart. Though, between you and me, the path with the most tea parties is usually the most fun!"

Whispers of the Dream Granter

Lily looked from one door to the other, her mind awash with memories. She thought of her family and friends in the ordinary world, the life she had left behind. But then she remembered all the wonders she had experienced in Bonbon Avenue, the magic she had discovered within herself, and the deep friendships she had forged.

As she pondered, her magical dress began to shimmer, replaying scenes from her adventures like a living tapestry. She saw herself solving riddles in the Whispering Woods, navigating the Midnight Maze, and riding the Carousel of Memories.

Felix casually painted stars in the air, which came to life and swirled around Lily's head. "No matter which door you choose," he said with a wink, "you'll still have to catch me in a game of sky-hopscotch!"

Wobbles, the frog tripped over the cobblestones as he offered advice: "Oh dear, I think the path to the ordinary world is slippery... or was it the magical one? Oh, how I do tumble about!"

Whispers of the Dream Granter

Twiggy Winkle, the mischievous pig, bounced up to Lily. "Whatever you choose, make sure it's full of tricks and treats! Life's too short for boring decisions!"

"Whatever you choose," Felix said, his usual mischievous grin replaced by a look of sincere affection, "know that you'll always be a part of Bonbon Avenue."

Benji's ears drooped slightly as he added, "And we'll always be a part of you."

Lily's hand closed around the Key of Wishes, feeling its warmth and energy. She took a deep breath, ready to make her choice.

But just as she was about to step towards one of the doors, a gust of wind swept through the gathering. The pages of an unseen book ruffled, and a new voice spoke, one that seemed to come from the very fabric of Bonbon Avenue itself.

"Wait, young Wishkeeper," the voice said, rich with wisdom and magic. "There is another path, one that has never been offered before."

A third door appeared, different from the others. It was neither fully of the ordinary world nor entirely of Bonbon

Avenue. Instead, it seemed to be a perfect blend of both. It changed shape continuously one moment, a simple bedroom door, the next covered in dancing mushrooms and stars that floated off into the sky.

This new door spoke in a dreamy voice, "I am the path less chosen, the road of both and neither. To open me, you must first answer the question: What happens when two wishes collide?" It playfully moved sideways, laughing, "I'm here! No, wait, I'm there! Oh, it's so much fun to be everything at once!"

"This door," the voice continued, "leads to a life where you can be a bridge between worlds. You would have the power to visit Bonbon Avenue whenever you wish, bringing its magic to your ordinary life and sharing the wonders of your world with us."

Lily's eyes widened at this unexpected option. She looked to her friends, seeing hope rekindled in their eyes.

Penny offered her cryptic, playful wisdom: "One path is filled with certainty, but oh, how boring certainty can be! The other is filled with wonder, but be careful it has a tendency to nibble on your sanity! Or perhaps you'll take the one that whispers secrets in the language of dreams?"

Sophie Willowtail handed Lily a magical spool of thread, saying, "In case you choose the ordinary door, this will help you sew a bit of magic into it!"

Mr. Crumbles offered her an ever-changing cupcake: "Each bite is a different flavor, and no matter which door you go through, you'll always have a taste of adventure with you!"

"The choice remains yours," the voice concluded. "But know that true magic lies not in choosing one world over another, but in finding the wonder that exists in all realms."

With this new possibility before her, Lily felt her heart swell with emotion. She looked at the Key of Wishes, then at each of the three doors, understanding that this moment would define not just her future, but the future of Bonbon Avenue as well.

As she prepared to make her decision, Lily realized that her greatest adventure wasn't ending, it was just beginning. Whatever she chose, she knew that the magic she had discovered in Bonbon Avenue would be a part of her forever.

Whispers of the Dream Granter

With a deep breath and a heart full of love for both worlds, Lily raised the Key of Wishes, ready to unlock the next chapter of her extraordinary journey. As she did, the world tilted at an impossible angle, with stars sliding down the sky like water and the ground bubbling like tea.

"Oops!" the ground said, "A little excited there, aren't we?"

As Lily raised the Key of Wishes, ready to make her choice, a sudden wave of dizziness washed over her. The world of Bonbon Avenue began to blur and swirl around her, colors melding together in a kaleidoscope of magic and memory.

She blinked, and when she opened her eyes, she found herself in a familiar place, her own bedroom in the ordinary world. Sunlight streamed through the window, and the sounds of a typical morning drifted in from outside.

For a moment, Lily lay still, her heart racing. Had it all been a dream? The magical village, her whimsical friends, the incredible adventures, were they nothing more than figments of her imagination?

As she sat up, something caught her eye. There, arranged neatly on her bed, were plush toys she had never seen before.

Whispers of the Dream Granter

A white rabbit wearing a simple white dress with a cream-colored cardigan and a yellow bow tied neatly around her neck, a mischievous-looking fox, a clumsy frog, a squirrel with twinkling eyes, and many more, each one a perfect representation of her friends from Bonbon Avenue.

Lily reached out and picked up the white rabbit plush, her fingers gently touching the soft yellow bow as she hugged it close. As she did, she felt something hard inside the toy. Curious, she reached into a hidden pocket in the rabbit's cardigan and pulled out a small, glittering object.

It was the Key of Wishes, just as magical and otherworldly as she remembered.

A smile spread across Lily's face as she looked at the key, then at the array of plush toys surrounding her. Perhaps the line between dreams and reality, between the ordinary and the magical, was more blurred than she had ever imagined.

As she clutched the key and the white rabbit plush to her chest, Lily knew that her adventures in Bonbon Avenue were far from over. They were, in fact, just beginning.

Whispers of the Dream Granter

With her heart full of excitement and wonder, Lily jumped out of bed, ready to discover how the magic of Bonbon Avenue would blend with her everyday world. After all, as she had learned, true magic exists everywhere... if you only know how to look for it.

THE END

Beneath the boughs, so soft and bright,

The Dream Tree whispers in the night.

Its leaves aglow, a starry veil,

Where wishes dance, and dreams set sail.

The gentle breeze begins to hum

A lullaby for what's to come.

For in the stillness, hearts take flight,

And hopes awaken in the light.

Each wish we hold, so pure, so true,

Floats up to where the stars debut.

And as the Dream Tree sways with grace,

Our longings bloom in starlit space.

Oh, Dream Tree, wise and old as time,

You turn our whispers into rhyme.

With every leaf that falls from thee,

A dream is born a destiny

So let us sit beneath your shade,

Where every hope and wish is made.

For in your arms, we find the key,

The magic of what's meant to be.

www.ingramcontent.com/pod-product-compliance
Ingram Content Group UK Ltd.
Pitfield, Milton Keynes, MK11 3LW, UK
UKHW051152171125
9002UKWH00006B/19